P9-BHZ-398

Level D

Reading Explorations

Globe Fearon

Writers: Joanne Suter and Sandra Widener
Senior Editor: Nance Davidson
Project Editors: Marion Castellucci, Amy Jolin,
    Robert McIlwaine
Editorial Assistant: Marilyn Bashoff
Production Editor: Rosann Bar
Electronic Page Production: Heather Roake
Electronic Art: Armando Baez

Printed in the United States of America
  3 4 5 6 7 8 9 10   01 00 99 98

ISBN 0-835-93443-8

Globe Fearon Educational Publisher
A Division of Simon & Schuster
Upper Saddle River, New Jersey

Contents

Social Studies

Step back in time. You're about to visit some interesting places. You're going to meet some interesting people.

King Tut's Tomb

Tutankhamen died thousands of years ago. Scientists later found his **tomb.** It was an important discovery. The tomb was full of riches. Today, it is still a wonder.

Tutankhamen became king of Egypt when he was still a boy. He is called King Tut for short. He ruled more than 3,300 years ago. Because he was so young, he is sometimes called "the boy king." King Tut died when he was only 18.

In his day, people did a special thing when a king died. They buried him in a tomb. The tomb was as big as a house. It had many rooms. The king's gold and other treasures were buried with him.

King Tut was buried in Egypt's Valley of the Kings. There were 30 tombs there. The tombs were covered with sand to hide them. It was thought that no one could find the tombs.

Many years went by. People did find the tombs. They stole many of the treasures. Only one tomb stayed hidden. That was the tomb of King Tut. It stayed hidden for 3,200 years!

1. What was buried in a king's tomb with him?

2. Where was King Tut's tomb?

Then, in 1907, an English scientist named Howard Carter went to Egypt. He was looking for things people made long ago. He was working for an Englishman named Lord Carnavon. Together they began to search for King Tut's tomb. For 15 years they found nothing.

Then, in November 1922, Carter reached the door to King Tut's tomb. He dug some more. Then he came to another door. He cut a small hole in it. He stuck a candle through the hole. What he saw inside amazed him.

The room was filled with gold and other riches. Carter had found the treasure of King Tut! Soon Carter and his men found other rooms. They found more treasure. They continued to dig for 10 more years. In all, they found more than 5,000 things.

Carter and his men found many wonderful treasures. They found jewelry and weapons. They found statues and paintings. They even found furniture. Many of these things were made of gold.

In 1925, Carter found the **coffin** of King Tut. It was in a nest of golden coffins. Inside the smallest box was the boy king's body. It had been kept as a **mummy,** wrapped in cloth.

The news of Carter's find spread. He came to the United States to speak. He even met the president. Carter became famous all over the world.

The boy king became famous, too. People started wearing King Tut hats. They wore King Tut rings. Women wore King Tut dresses. Almost everything that looked Egyptian became popular. Someone even named a cigar after King Tut.

More than 50 years passed. Then King Tut was in the news again. The treasures of his tomb were sent around the world for people to see. King Tut's treasures came to the United States. Thousands of people saw them in museums. They stood in line for hours. They waited to see the treasures. People were excited. They were thrilled. They got to see riches from a long-ago time. They learned about King Tut, the boy king who was hidden for more than 3,200 years!

3. Why do you think people long ago buried kings in tombs full of treasures? What does this tell you about their ideas of life after death?

4. What did the people long ago do to King Tut's dead body to keep it in good shape?

5. Why do you think people were excited about seeing King Tut's treasures?

The Wright Brothers

WORDS TO KNOW

Ohio (oh-HEYE-oh) a state in the middle part of the United States

North Carolina (nawrth kair-oh-LEYE-nuh) a state in the southern part of the United States

invention (ihn-VEHN-shuhn) a thing or a way of doing something that has never been made or thought of before

glider (GLEYE-duhr) a light aircraft without an engine. It floats on the air and moves with the wind.

For thousands of years, people watched the birds and wished they could fly. Finally, in 1903, two brothers made a dream come true. They made and flew the first airplane.

There were two brothers who worked in a bicycle shop. Their home was in **Ohio.** Now the brothers were far from home. They were on a beach in **North Carolina.** It was December 1903. But they were not there to swim in the ocean. They were there to fly.

The brothers were Orville and Wilbur Wright. They had made an **invention.** It was the first flying machine. It was the first airplane with an engine. The airplane was supposed to take a person up into the air with power from its engine. Then it would land. That had never been done before.

The brothers had built the airplane, or plane, in their bicycle shop. The plane weighed about 600 pounds. Its wings were about 40 feet across. The two men also built the engine. It ran on gasoline. They spent $1,000 of their own money to make this flying machine.

1. What did the Wright brothers invent?

2. Describe two things about the Wright brothers' invention.

They were ready to test the machine. Wilbur tried to fly it. The airplane barely lifted off the ground. The engine stalled. It stopped running. It lost power. The plane fell to the ground. It had been in the air for just 3 seconds.

Still, the brothers wanted to try again. Nothing would stop them. The next day, the weather was bad. It was very cold. The wind was blowing hard off the ocean. They still wanted to try to fly the airplane.

The men pointed the plane into the wind. Then Orville climbed out onto the lower wing and stretched out face down. Wilbur tied a strap around him so he would not fall off.

Wilbur started the engine. Orville grabbed the plane's controls. It went straight into the wind.

Slowly, the plane began to rise into the air. It went higher and higher. It reached 10 feet in the air. Someone on the beach shouted, "He's flying! He's flying!"

A few moments later, the plane landed. Wilbur checked his stopwatch. It counted every second. His brother had been in the air for a full 12 seconds! The airplane had gone about 120 feet in the air.

Other people had used a **glider** to travel that far before. Even the Wright brothers had flown gliders. A glider floats on the air. It has no engine. Orville's first flight was different, though.

Gliders could fly from a high hill to a lower place by using the wind. Orville's plane used engine power. It started on a tall hill and landed on another equally tall hill. No one had ever done that before.

The brothers kept flying that day. Wilbur took a turn and flew over 800 feet. He stayed in the air almost a full minute. Then their luck changed. A strong wind came up. It tipped the plane over. The plane was damaged. It would not run on its own power. It would not fly. It had to be fixed.

That was all right, though. The brothers knew they could fix it. They knew they could make it better. This was just the beginning of flight. Wilbur and Orville Wright were the first people to fly.

3. What happened when the Wright brothers first tried to fly and failed?

4. What is the difference between an airplane and a glider?

5. What are two ways the second flight was better than the first flight?

6. Why were the Wright Brothers not upset when their plane got damaged?

7. What kind of people were the Wright Brothers? How did they feel about mistakes or failures?

Immigrants

People sometimes move to a new country. They may not have good jobs at home. They may want to join other family members. They may want more freedom. These people make a new life in their new country. They are called **immigrants.**

The United States is a home for immigrants. People come here from all over the world. They come from **Europe.** They come from **Asia.** Many are young. Some are poor.

From 1890 to 1920, about 18 million people came to our country. Most were from Europe or Asia. Many came from England, Ireland, and Italy. These are countries in Europe. Millions of people came from China, a huge country in Asia.

Most people had a hard time getting here. Ships were slow. They were crowded. When they got here, they did not have a home to go to.

Immigrants were checked. U.S. workers looked at their papers. The immigrants had to answer questions. Some were turned away because they couldn't answer. Others had done crimes. They were sent back home.

1. Name two countries that immigrants to the United States came from.

2. Name one reason that some immigrants were sent back.

Still, millions were allowed to stay. Many went to large cities. In these cities, immigrants often lived near each other. Irish people lived together. So did the Italian people. By living close, they could speak their own language. They could keep their **customs.** They could wear their own style of dress. They could cook food their own way.

Many immigrants were poor. They had to find work. It was not easy. Many could not speak English well. They had to take the lowest paid jobs.

Some people in the U.S. felt immigrants took jobs from U.S. workers. This was not true. Immigrants did jobs no one else wanted. They sewed clothes. They worked in mines. They cleaned houses. They worked in factories.

Still, many Americans did not like the immigrants. After 1920, the law about immigrants changed. Congress passed new laws. One new law said immigrants must know how to read. Another said only a certain number of people would be let in each year.

Still, many immigrants did well. Some became leaders. Some opened businesses. Their children were born here.

People from all over the world live together here. They work together. Their children go to school together. They are neighbors. Some go to the same churches. They learn our customs. They vote. They all become one people: Americans.

3. Why did many immigrants live near people who came from the same countries they came from?

4. What was one new thing that the laws after 1920 said about immigrants?

5. Some people said that immigrants took jobs away from U.S. workers. Why is this not true?

6. Describe how immigrants become Americans.

Rosa Parks

For over 100 years, African Americans did not
have the same rights as white Americans.
Then, in the 1950s, one woman helped to
change all that.

Rosa Parks lived in **Alabama.** She was African American. It was a bad time for African Americans in the South. They did not have the same rights as white people. They had to sit at the back of buses. They had to drink out of special drinking fountains. There were a lot of angry African Americans in the South.

On December 1, 1955, Rosa Parks was tired. It had been a long day. She climbed onto the bus. Her feet hurt, so she sat down in the first seat she came to. It was in the front of the bus. She closed her eyes and tried to rest.

The bus moved on. It stopped, again and again. Soon, all the seats were full.

A white man got on. There were no empty seats. He looked at the bus driver. The driver told Rosa Parks to give the man her seat. Rosa Parks didn't feel like standing because she was very tired. Also, she didn't think it was fair.

"Get up!" the bus driver yelled. "No," she said.

Rosa Parks broke a law. The law said she must give her seat to a white person. The driver reported her to the police. She was arrested. She paid $100 in bail. She was free for a while.

1. Why were the 1950s a bad time for African Americans in the south?

2. Where did Rosa Parks sit on the bus?

A court date was set. Rosa Parks wondered if they would send her to jail. She did not know what she had done wrong. All she did was stay in her seat. She did not know why that was wrong. Rosa Parks wanted to fight the law. But she did not know how.

A young minister had an idea. He was a church leader. His name was **Martin Luther King, Jr.** He spoke in church. "Anger won't work," he said. "We have to change the law. We have to show the world what is going on. Let's **boycott** the buses. Let's not ride on them. This law **discriminates.** It is not fair."

King and the other ministers put up notices. They invited everyone to come to church on Sunday. They planned to discuss the boycott.

On Sunday, all the churches were packed. King told people about the boycott. The next day, African Americans stayed off the buses.

They walked to work. People started car pools. Many whites helped. The buses were almost empty. The boycott continued for more than a year. The city was losing a lot of money. The boycott was working.

In the meantime, Rosa Parks didn't quit. She went to court. She fought the law.

"Let's **appeal**," she told her lawyer. "Let's take it to a higher court."

Rosa Parks's lawyer appealed. The judge said the law was legal. Her lawyer appealed to an even higher court. The judge said, "It is legal to keep people apart on buses."

Rosa Parks still didn't quit. There was one court left. Her lawyer took her case to the U.S. Supreme Court. At last, the top court in the land decided. The judges said, "This law is not legal. No one should have to give up a seat because of race. No one has to sit in the back of the bus because of race."

Rosa Parks had made a change. All she did was stay in her seat. But it was much more than that. Rosa Parks showed people how to stand up for what they believed in.

3. Why do you think the South made laws that separated African Americans from white Americans?

4. If you wanted to boycott a local store, what might you do?

5. How does a boycott make changes happen?

6. What was Rosa Parks doing while the bus boycott was going on?

7. How did Rosa Parks's refusal to sit in the back of the bus help other African Americans?

Nelson Mandela

WORDS TO KNOW

Nelson Mandela (NEHL-suhn man-DEHL-uh)
the main African leader against apartheid

township (TOWN-shihp) in South Africa,
places where most blacks had to live

apartheid (uh-PAHR-tyt) laws that kept races
apart from each other in South Africa

nonviolent (nahn-VY-oh-lehnt) peaceful

F.W. de Klerk (ehf DUHB-uhl-yoo duh-KLERK)
one of the white presidents of South
Africa

Some laws are unfair. They don't consider the
rights of others. **Nelson Mandela** fought
against unfair laws in South Africa.

South Africa is a country in the southern part of Africa. Life there is based on people's race.

Black Africans were likely to live in a **township.** Townships were poor. Many had no running water. They had no electricity. The schools had few books. To leave the township, people needed a pass. They might need a pass to go to work. They were only allowed to work at some jobs.

Whites in South Africa were much better off. They were few in number but they had power. They owned most businesses. They owned land. People of other races worked for them. They made laws that kept people apart. These laws were called **apartheid.**

Many people in South Africa thought apartheid was wrong. They wanted to end it. They wanted fair laws. They wanted a say in running their country.

One man who fought apartheid was Nelson Mandela. Mandela was a black South African. He led the African National Congress.

The group's short name was ANC. ANC comes from the first letters of **A**frican **N**ational **C**ongress.

The ANC was a group of black South Africans. They wanted to make life better for blacks. They worked against apartheid.

1. What was apartheid?

2. What was the ANC?

In 1951, Mandela and the ANC made a plan. They wanted to force whites to change the laws. If the laws were not changed, the ANC would take **nonviolent** action. The action would be peaceful. But it would make life for whites hard.

The whites said they would not change the laws. In 1952, blacks began a nonviolent action. It upset the country. Blacks did not go to work. They marched into places for whites only. At night, they stayed out later than the law allowed.

The whites jailed many people. Riots started. People were killed. Mandela was jailed for the first time.

The ANC kept up nonviolent actions for years. In 1960, a nonviolent action turned ugly. The police killed many blacks. The whites in power said the ANC was against the law. They said it could not exist.

This was a turning point. For years Mandela and the ANC had been nonviolent. Now it was time for violence. In 1961, Mandela's group began attacking the government. Now they used guns.

Mandela and other leaders were caught. The ANC leaders were put on trial. Mandela and seven others were found guilty. In 1964, they were sent to jail for life.

More years went by. The ANC still worked against apartheid. From jail, Mandela led them. There was more violence.

Meanwhile, the world watched South Africa. Many countries turned against it. They thought apartheid was wrong. They said it should end. Mandela should be free. They would not sell things to South Africa. They would not buy things from South Africa.

Still, the government would not give in.

In the late 1980s, people all over the world were saying "Free Mandela." Violence continued. Blacks burned government offices. Police killed both blacks and whites. South Africa was out of control.

In 1989, a new white president came to power. His name was **F. W. de Klerk.** He saw that apartheid had to end. He said Mandela would go free.

On February 11, 1990, Mandela left jail. He was free for the first time in almost 28 years. He was 71 years old. A crowd waited for him. Everyone cheered.

Mandela met often with de Klerk. They worked to bring peace to their country. In 1993, they agreed to hold a free election. All South Africans would be able to vote.

In 1994, the first free election in South Africa's history was held. The ANC got more than half the vote. Mandela was elected president. The long fight for freedom had been won.

3. What was life in South Africa like for blacks during apartheid?

4. Describe the way nonviolent action was used to fight apartheid.

5. Explain why black South Africans turned to nonviolent action in 1952.

6. Why did the ANC decide to turn to violence in 1961?

7. How did some other countries fight against apartheid in South Africa?

8. How did Mandela become president?

Science

The readings in this section have something in common. All of them are about people or things that happen in the air.

Bats

WORDS TO KNOW

echoes (EHK-ohz) sounds that repeat after bouncing off something

mammals (MAM-uhlz) animals with warm blood, backbones, and often, fur. They feed their babies with milk from their own bodies.

hibernate (HEYE-buhr-nayt) to spend the winter sleeping or staying inside

migrate (MEYE-grayt) to move from one place to another when the seasons change

vampire bat (VAM-peyer bat) a kind of bat that feeds on blood

Stories and movies have made them seem like scary animals. We forget they also do important things.

Many people never even see bats. That's because bats hide during the day. They sleep while it is light outside.

Bats are good at finding their way in the dark. They use parts of their nose, mouth, and ears to see. But they are not really seeing. They are using sounds to find their way.

Here's how it works. A bat sends out very high sounds through its nose or mouth. These sounds bounce off anything that is near. The sounds come back to the bat as **echoes.** They are heard by the nose and ears. By hearing the echoes, the bat can tell where things are. In this way, the bat can keep from flying into them.

Bats are **mammals.** They have backbones, arms, hands, legs, and feet. Their bodies are covered with fur. They fly, but they are not birds. The wings of bats are covered with skin, not feathers. Each wing goes from the bat's hand to its tail. The bat's wings can be bigger than its body. With these wings, a bat can fly very fast. Bats are the only mammals that fly.

1. How do bats find their way in the dark?

2. Name two things that make bats mammals.

Bats come in many sizes. Some bats are less than an inch long. Others are more than a foot long. Some bats spread their wings a few inches. Others have wings that are 5 feet from tip to tip!

Bats eat many things. Some feed on insects.

Others eat fruit. Some bats eat small mammals or birds. They may eat frogs or fish.

Bats usually live in caves or trees. They can also be found in dark places in buildings. Some bats live around a home or garden. These small, brown bats are called common bats. They stay in the same place all year round.

During cold weather, some kinds of bats **hibernate.** They sleep all winter in a warm place like a cave. Other bats **migrate** when cold weather starts. They fly to a warmer place for the winter.

The movies have given bats a bad name. A movie might show a bat biting a person. This person suddenly changes into a bat. This does not happen in real life. People do not change into bats!

Still, some bats *are* dangerous. The **vampire bat** is one of them. It has very sharp, long teeth. The vampire bat has a very narrow throat. It must drink its food. The only thing it eats is blood.

To eat, the vampire bat bites an animal.

The bite makes the animal bleed. The vampire bat drinks the blood.

Vampire bats often have diseases. Anything they bite can get those diseases.

Other kinds of bats are not dangerous. They help us in many ways. Bats carry seeds. When they drop the seeds, new plants grow. Bats also eat bugs. Many of these bugs would hurt the flowers and vegetables growing in the fields. Other bugs like mosquitos would bite people. But bats make our lives better by eating the bugs first.

3. What is one difference between a bat and a bird?

4. Name two things that bats eat.

5. What does a bat do when it hibernates?

6. How does a vampire bat feed itself?

7. Why are many people afraid of bats?

8. How do bats help people?

When Birds Migrate

WORDS TO KNOW

nesting grounds (NEHST-ihng growndz)
where birds lay eggs and raise their young

flock (flahk) a group of animals or birds that
live, travel, or feed together

routes (rootz) ways to go to a certain place

deserts (DEH-zuhrts) hot, dry, sandy places

coasts (kohstz) edges of land by oceans

snow geese (snoh gees) birds from Canada

The days get shorter and colder in the fall.
Birds don't like to hang around. Instead, they fly
south where it is warmer.

Flying south isn't hard for birds. They may have to fly hundreds or thousands of miles. But they know exactly where they are going. They went to the same place last year. They will go to the same place next year.

The birds leave their **nesting grounds.** That's where they laid eggs and raised their babies during spring and summer.

Not all birds migrate. Some birds live all year round in the same place. Other birds take long trips twice each year. One trip is usually made in the early fall. The other is made in the early spring.

Birds always know when it's time to migrate in the fall. Their bodies begin to change. They lose old feathers and grow new ones. They store extra fat on their bodies. They begin to get restless at night. They know it is time to head to their winter homes.

1. What are nesting grounds?

2. How do birds know when it is time to migrate?

Some birds get ready to go in a large group called a **flock.** They feed together for many days before they leave. Then they travel together. Robins fly in flocks.

Other birds fly on their long trips alone. Hummingbirds fly by themselves. They are the smallest American bird.

All birds that migrate follow certain **routes.** They fly the same ways every year. They don't fly over mountains. They usually stay away from large **deserts.** They don't fly over large bodies of water.

Instead, many birds fly along the **coasts** of oceans. Others fly along the sides of large lakes. Some birds fly along the sides of mountains. Others fly above large rivers. They need to be able to drink water often.

Small birds usually migrate during the night. Most fly from a few hundred to a few thousand feet in the air. Many large birds fly during the day. These birds can fly thousands of feet up in the sky.

Some birds fly only 200 to 400 miles at a time. Then they rest. They stay in one place for a while. They build up more fat on their bodies. Then they are ready to continue their long trip.

Other birds make one very long flight. **Snow geese** live in a part of Canada. Canada is the country north of the United States. They migrate to the southeastern United States. The trip is about 1,700 miles. The geese fly 60 hours without stopping. Now, *that's* flying.

People often wonder how birds can tell direction. They want to know how they take the same route each year. They want to know how they get to the same place each year.

Birds use many things to help them tell direction. They use the mountains and valleys. They use the position of the sun in the sky. They use the stars at night. They use the direction of the wind.

The birds spend the whole winter in warm places. When spring comes, they get ready to return home. Once again they grow new feathers.

They store extra fat on their bodies. Then they head off into the sky.

Finally, they reach their nesting grounds. For the next few months, this will be home. Then once more, fall arrives. The long journey south begins all over again.

3. Why do you think many birds migrate in flocks?

4. Name two types of places that birds fly over when they migrate.

5. Why do you think many birds do not fly over large deserts when they migrate?

6. What do birds do when they stop on a long trip?

7. Name two things birds use to help them tell direction when they fly.

Mount Everest

It rises more than 29,000 feet in the air. It is the
highest mountain in the world. Its name is
Mount Everest.

Five miles is a very long distance. Imagine something more than five miles high. That's how high the top of Mount Everest is.

Mount Everest is the highest mountain in the world. It is part of a very large group of mountains called the **Himalayas.** The Himalayas cover about 1,500 miles. They are in Asia.

Mount Everest is a great challenge to people who climb mountains. Climbing to the top is a very difficult job. The weather is bitter cold. The winds always blow very hard. Breathing at the top is almost impossible. The air is very thin at such heights. Climbers bring **oxygen** with them so they can breathe.

1. To which mountain range does Mount Everest belong?

2. Name two things that make climbing Mount Everest very difficult.

For a long time, no one could even try to climb Mount Everest. The area was closed to travelers. Then, in 1921, a group of English explorers went in. They were allowed to try to climb the mountain. They made it to 22,900 feet. A year later, another group made it to 27,000 feet. Still, no one had reached the top.

These trips were very dangerous. On one climb, seven people died. They were killed in an **avalanche.** Tons of snow slid down the mountain and buried them. Two men disappeared as they were trying to reach the top. Other climbers became very sick.

More than 20 years passed. Now climbers were trying to reach the top of Mount Everest from the south. In 1952, two men got to more than 28,000 feet.

An Englishman named **Edmund Hillary** tried to climb Mount Everest twice. He had his chief guide with him. His name was **Tenzing Norgay.** He knew Mount Everest well. He knew a lot about climbing mountains. Still, they failed to reach the top both times.

In 1953, Hillary decided to try Mount Everest once more. Hillary, Norgay, and a large group set out in March. Their team had more than 300 men. They carried 10,000 pounds of food and other things with them.

At times the weather was bad. It was a long, slow climb. They climbed for 80 days. Finally, on May 29, Hillary and Norgay made one last climb. Then they looked around. Above them was only the sky. They had done it. They had reached the top of the highest mountain in the world!

Since 1953, there have been more trips. Mountain climbers have found new ways to get to the top. In 1963, one group went across the top of Mount Everest. They climbed up one side of the mountain. Then they climbed down on another side.

There have been other events on Mount Everest. In 1975, the first woman reached the top. In 1978, two men made the climb without using extra oxygen. In 1980, one of these men climbed Mount Everest alone. He was the first person ever to reach the top by himself.

The mountain reaches more than 5 miles into the sky. Hundreds of people have tried to get there. Many have died. But for the lucky ones, there is a reward. They can say, "I climbed to the top of Mount Everest. I was on top of the world."

3. What is one danger of climbing Mount Everest?

4. Who were the first people to climb to the top of Mount Everest?

5. What are two "first-time events" that climbers have done since 1953?

6. Why do you think people want to climb Mount Everest?

Rocket Man

WORDS TO KNOW

rocket (RAHK-iht) a thing that burns fuel to make a jet of gas, which pushes it forward and upward so that it flies

fuel (FYOO-uhl) something burned to make heat or light, or to make a machine move

experiments (ehk-SPEHR-uh-muhntz) tests to see if a thing or idea works

research (REE-surch) careful study of something to find out facts about it

orbit (AWR-biht) the path of anything around another thing in space

Have you ever wondered how a **rocket** works? This is the story of a man who spent his life making better and better rockets.

It was July 20, 1969. The world was amazed. People everywhere were thrilled. The United States had sent a rocket to the moon. Soon, two men would walk on the moon. Some said it was the most important event in history.

Robert H. Goddard did not live to see men land on the moon. He died in 1945. But if he had lived, Goddard would have smiled. Maybe he would have said four short words: "I told you so." That's because many of Goddard's ideas about rockets were used in that flight to the moon. Goddard was the "rocket man." Here is his story.

Robert Goddard was born in 1882. Growing up, he was interested in space flight. He graduated from college in 1908. The next year, he began writing down his ideas. He had ideas about **fuel** for rockets. He had ideas about engines for rockets. He had ideas about how to send a rocket to the moon.

Goddard became a college teacher. He tried many **experiments.** Some of these tests used small rocket engines. In 1919, he wrote a report about rockets. He told what it would take to send a rocket to the moon.

Many people read the report. A lot of them did not believe it. Some people did not believe people could fly a rocket on Earth. Who was crazy enough to think people could fly to the moon?

Still, Goddard had some support. Some scientists believed his ideas were right. He got money to continue his **research.** This time he decided to keep his studies secret. He wasn't sure the world was ready for his ideas.

Goddard began working with liquid fuels. Liquid fuels are like gasoline. They can be poured. By 1926, he was ready. That year, he launched a rocket. It used liquid fuel. The rocket traveled 184 feet. It went more than 60 miles an hour. It was the first time anyone had used liquid fuel to launch a rocket.

1. What was Goddard's 1919 report about?

2. What type of fuel did Goddard use in his 1926 rocket?

Before 1926, all rockets used solid fuel. The fuel was made of a hard material like gunpowder. When solid fuel is lit, it all burns until there is none left. The burning cannot be stopped or slowed down. This means that the rocket can't be stopped or slowed down either. Fireworks are simple solid fuel rockets. Once you light them, they go!

Liquid fuels are important. Their burning can be stopped or slowed inside the rocket engine. That means the speed of the rocket can be changed. More fuel in the engine makes the rocket go faster. Less fuel slows it down. Goddard's 1926 rocket pointed the way to better rocket engines.

Goddard kept working on rockets. He tried more tests. Years passed. In 1930, he tested a new rocket. It used liquid oxygen and gasoline. It flew 2,000 feet. It went 500 miles an hour.

During the next few years, Goddard launched more rockets. A team of people helped him. They made films of their launches. One day Goddard called in some news people. He wanted to show them what he'd been doing.

The news people watched the films. They were amazed. They saw rockets 11 feet long. They weighed up to 85 pounds. They reached as high as 4,000 feet. Black smoke marked their paths in the sky. Fifteen years before, many people had laughed at Goddard. Now he proved that his rockets worked.

Goddard kept writing about his work. He kept testing more rockets. He did more work with fuels and engines. Then the United States asked him for help.

World War II had started. Goddard went to work for the U.S. Navy. They wanted to make faster and better planes. They thought his ideas about rocket engines could be helpful. Goddard did research for them.

Robert Goddard died just as the war ended in 1945. Then came the 1950s. Goddard's ideas were put into action. Russia, a large country in Europe and Asia, had its own rockets. Russia and the United States began a race to put men in outer space. They launched rockets. They sent them into **orbit,** circling the Earth.

In the 1960s, more rockets took off. Now there were men aboard them. Soon the United States made a promise. It would send a rocket and men to the moon and back. By now many people thought it could be done.

In 1969, the United States kept its promise. A rocket with several men went to the moon. Fifty years earlier, Robert Goddard had said it could be done. Back then, many people laughed. In 1969, no one was laughing. They were cheering. Many of the cheers were for Robert Goddard.

3. What did Robert Goddard work on for the U.S. Navy?

4. How are liquid fuels different from solid fuels?

5. Why was liquid fuel better for rockets?

6. Where in space did the United States send men in a rocket?

Math

Math comes in handy. It helps you to take polls or estimate crowds. It helps you to figure out your diet or the best time to make long distance calls.

Polls

WORDS TO KNOW

poll (pohl) a way to find out what people think by asking questions of a small number of people in a group. Their answers stand for the answers of the whole group.

represent (reh-prih-ZEHNT) to stand for; to be an example of something larger

sample (SAM-puhl) a small group of different types of people who represent all the types in a larger group

politician (pahl-ih-TISH-uhn) a person holding a public office, such as a mayor

Do you want to know what people in general think about something? You can't ask all of them. You have to choose a small number to ask. If you ask different types of people in the group, you can get a good idea of what the whole group thinks.

Kim's school is having an election for student body president. Everyone wants to know who will win. Kim decides to find the answer. How can he do this? He can't ask everyone. That would be too hard. It would take too long. What he does instead is take a **poll.**

Poll takers ask people what they think. Then they count the answers. Kim could ask five of his friends. Will their answers tell him the winner? Probably not. All his friends might be boys. They all might be seniors. That would not tell him what other kinds of students in the school think.

Kim needs to ask different kinds of students. How can he do this? First, he will sit down and make a list of the groups of people in his school. There are girls and boys. There are people of different classes, from freshmen to seniors. There are people who like sports better than school. There are people who like school better than sports. Kim looks at his list. He thinks he has every main group in the school.

Kim wants to make sure he has all the main groups, though. He asks someone else to look at the list. This person reminds Kim that people who go to their school live in different parts of town. He adds those groups to the list. He adds the group of people who live in one part of town. He adds the group of people who live in another part of town.

1. What is the reason for taking a poll?

2. How do poll takers make sure they ask different kinds of people?

Now Kim has his list of groups. The next step is asking five people in each group.

Kim hopes the answers of the students from each group will tell him whom the members of each group will vote for. The five students' answers stand for, or **represent,** what each group thinks.

Do these people really think the same as others in the same group? Maybe they do. Maybe they don't. The answers of people in a group are more likely to be the same than if Kim asked just anyone, though. The answers of some people in a group can give poll takers a fairly good idea of what that group thinks.

Kim has taken his poll. He asked five people from every group he could think of. Will his poll be right? That depends on his list of groups. Did he really have all the main groups in the school? Let's say he asked only boys. He would have left out a big group of girls. He needs students from all the groups to make his poll right.

If Kim asked students from all the important groups, he will have a **sample** of the school. That means he has a small group of different types. That small group stands for the larger group, the school. If Kim has done this, his poll is likely to be right.

Poll taking is an important job. Many people want to find out what others think. Companies want to find out what people will buy. For example, a candy company may want to know if people like soft or hard candy. A **politician** may want to know if people will vote for him. Someone who makes movies may wonder if people like a certain movie star.

With so much polling going on, be prepared.

Someday soon you may get a call. "Hello," a person will say. "Do you have a minute? I'm taking a poll."

3. What is a sample?

4. Name two smaller groups that are part of the whole group in your class.

5. How can a poll taker decide whether the poll has been done well?

6. Why is poll taking an important job?

7. Name one group that uses polls. What do they want to find out?

Counting Crowds

WORDS TO KNOW

reporters (ree-PAWRT-erz) news people

promoters (pruh-moht-erz) people who hold an event like a concert

grid (grihd) lines that form boxes. One set of lines goes across. The other set of lines goes up and down. Each of the lines is the same distance apart.

How many people are in a big crowd? There's a special way to count them. Read this to find out how it's done.

People came to the park all day long. They wanted to hear the concert that night. It was free. They came early to get good seats.

By 8 P.M., thousands of people were there. The music began. **Reporters,** or news people, from a TV station were there. The concert would be on the news that night. The TV people asked, "How many people are here tonight?"

The **promoters,** or people who put on the concert, said there were 2,000 people. The police said there were 900 people. Who was right?

The TV people decided to do their own count. They used a special way to count the people in a crowd.

Here is what they did. First, a camera man went up in a helicopter. He took a picture of the whole crowd. He took the picture from high above. The picture shows the tops of many people's heads.

Then another person from the station looked at the picture. She made sure the whole crowd was shown. Then she drew a **grid** over the picture. A grid is a set of lines. One set of

lines went across the picture. Another set of
lines went up and down. The lines in the grid
were all one inch apart. That is important. The
lines must form boxes that are all the same size.
If the lines are all one inch apart, the boxes
will be the same size. Here is how the picture
looked.

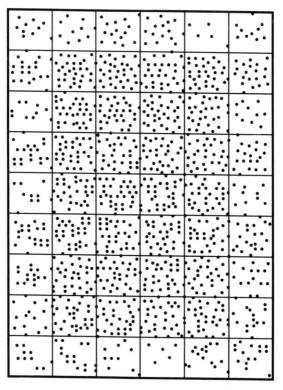

1. What is a grid?

2. Why should the lines be the same distance apart in a grid?

The crowd counter is ready to count. First she counts the people in the center of the crowd. She finds a box in the picture that is filled with many people. She counts the people in that box. There are 30 people in it.

Now she knows that in each box that has many people, there are about 30 people. She doesn't have to count all the people in all the boxes with many people. She just has to count how many boxes have many people. She counts 28 boxes that have many people.

She needs to know how many people are in all these boxes. She multiplies the number of boxes by the number of people in each box. She multiplies 28 by 30 and gets 840.

She is not through yet. Now she needs to count the people on the edges of the crowd. The boxes on the edges of the crowd are not full. In one of them, there are only 20 people. In another, there are only 10.

She counts the people in the outer boxes one by one. There are 26 outer boxes with just a few people in them. She counts them all. She finds there are 360 people in these boxes. These people are on the edges of the crowd.

Now she can find out how many people were in the whole crowd. She writes the number of people in the full boxes. That number is 840. She writes the number of people on the edges of the crowd. Those are the people she counted one by one. That number is 360.

She adds 840 and 360. Now she knows how many people were in the crowd. There were 1,200 people.

When the TV station tells about the concert that night, this is what they say. "There was a free concert in the park. Many people came. In fact, 1,200 people came."

The TV station did not have to take the word of the concert people or the police about how many people came. Their guesses were wrong. By doing a count, the station found out how many people were there.

Next time you are in a crowd outside, look up. There may be a helicopter there. It may be taking your picture. You may be part of the crowd count.

3. Are most crowds thicker in the center or on the edges?

4. How does the crowd counter count people on the edges of the crowd?

5. Why did the TV station make its own count of the crowd?

6. Why is using a grid a good way to tell the size of a crowd?

Fat in Your Diet

WORDS TO KNOW

gram (gram) a measure of weight. There are about 28 grams in an ounce.

nutrition facts (noo-TRIHSH-uhn fakts) labels on food packages that tell about what is in food

serving (SERV-ing) how much of a food a person eats at one time

Many people eat too much fat. This is one reason they gain weight. Find out how much fat you eat by counting the grams.

Jake wanted to eat better, so he went to his doctor. She told Jake he should eat more fruit and vegetables. He should eat fewer sweets. He should eat less fat.

"A teenage girl should eat about 70 **grams** of fat a day," said Jake's doctor. "A teenage boy like you needs to eat about 93 grams of fat a day." A gram is not very heavy. In fact, there are about 28 grams in 1 ounce.

"That's fine," Jake said. "But how can I tell how many grams of fat I eat?"

"You can find out in a few places," said the doctor. "Here is one place to look." She gave Jake a book that listed foods and how many grams of fat they had.

"The second place to look is on food cans, boxes, and bags. The **nutrition facts** chart says what's in the food. It tells you how many grams of fat the food has.

1. How much fat should a teenage girl eat each day?

2. How much fat should a teenage boy eat each day?

3. What do the nutrition facts on food labels tell you?

"Let's say you eat cookies," the doctor went on. "Look at the package. It says how many grams of fat are in one **serving** of those cookies." One serving of cookies may be two or three cookies.

"A third place to find out about fat is from restaurants. Many have nutrition facts about the foods they serve."

"Okay," said Jake. "But how do I keep track of the fat I eat?"

"You should write down the grams of fat you eat," the doctor said. "Each time you eat, write what you ate. Then find out how many grams of fat are in the food. At the end of the day, add up the grams of fat. You should be eating 93 grams or less of fat. That's the right amount for you."

Jake went home. The next day, he began keeping track of the fat he ate. For breakfast, he had two pieces of toast with butter. He had a big glass of orange juice. He had two eggs fried in butter. After breakfast, Jake listed the foods and their grams of fat. He added the grams. The total was 31 grams of fat for breakfast.

During the morning, Jake had an apple. In his book, he looked up how many grams of fat an apple has. He found that apples have no fat, so he wrote 0 on his list.

For lunch, Jake went to a fast–food place. He had a big hamburger, a large order of French fries, and a milkshake. Before he left, he got a list of nutrition facts from the person at the counter.

Jake looked up the foods he had eaten. He added the grams of fat for lunch. He had eaten 59 grams of fat! Jake was surprised. He had eaten a lot of fat at lunch. He added his grams of fat from breakfast to his grams of fat from lunch. He got 90 grams of fat. That was almost 93 grams, the amount he should eat in the whole day. He hadn't even eaten dinner yet.

Jake decided to have a dinner low in fat. He looked in his book for foods that had few grams of fat. He had lettuce and tomatoes. He had a banana. He had a chicken breast. He ate some bread without butter. Then he added his grams of fat for dinner. He had eaten only 5 grams of fat.

Jake added up his grams of fat from all day. He had eaten 95 grams of fat that day. He had eaten 2 more grams of fat than he should have. That wasn't bad for the first day, he thought. The next time he went to a fast–food place, he decided, he would look at the nutrition facts before he ate.

4. What is a serving?

5. In which meal did Jake eat the most fat?

6. How did Jake know how many grams of fat he ate during the day?

7. What kinds of foods are high in fat?

8. Name two foods low in fat.

Time Zones

California (kal-ih-FAWR-nee-uh) a state on the West Coast of the United States

New York (noo yawrk) a state on the East Coast of the United States

time zone (teyem zohn) an area where it is the same time

Utah (YOO-tah) a state in the western part of the United States

Iowa (EYE-uh-wuh) a state in the middle part of the United States

In different parts of the country, the time is different. That's important to know if you are planning to call or visit someplace else.

Sally's soccer team has just been named the best in **California.** She's thrilled. She decides to call her grandparents in **New York.**

When she calls, her grandparents are not happy to hear from her. "Don't you know what time it is?" her grandmother says. "It's 12 midnight! We'll talk to you tomorrow. We'll call you in the morning."

Sally hangs up. It's not 12 midnight where she is in California. It's 9 P.M. Sally has just learned what can happen when you don't think about time zones. A **time zone** is a place where it is the same time. Look at the map. You will see where U.S. time zones are.

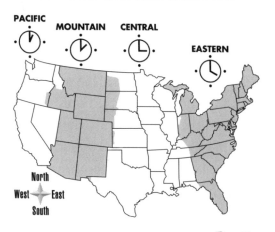

From the West Coast to the East Coast, there are four time zones. As you cross the United States from left to right on the map, each time you enter a new time zone it is one hour later.

Sally lives in California on the West Coast. She lives in Pacific time. Her grandparents live in New York on the East Coast. They live in Eastern time. When Sally called them, she was calling across three time zones. It is always three hours later in New York than in California.

1. What is a time zone?

2. What time was it in New York when it was 9 P.M. in California?

If Sally had called her cousin in **Utah** instead, it would have been 10 P.M. there. Sally's call would have crossed only one time zone. To find the time in Utah, Sally could look at the map. Her call would cross one time zone. So she would add one hour to the time in California. If it was 9 P.M. in California, it would be 10 P.M. in Utah. Utah is in Mountain time.

If Sally had called her aunt in **Iowa,** it would have been 11 P.M. there. Iowa is in Central time. Her aunt might have been sleeping. Sally could have found the time in Iowa by looking at the map. Calling from California to Iowa means crossing two time zones. To find the time in Iowa, Sally would add two hours. If it was 9 P.M. in California, it would be 11 P.M. in Iowa.

Let's say it's the next morning. Sally's grandparents want to call her back. They want to talk about her news. When they wake up, it is 7 A.M. in New York. What time is it in California?

To find the time in California, her grandparents look at the map. The call would go across three time zones. They need to subtract three hours from New York time. It is always three hours earlier in California than in New York. When it is 7 A.M. in New York, it is 4 A.M. in California. Sally is probably asleep.

"Too early to call," her grandfather says. "Let's wait a few hours. We want Sally to be awake when we tell her how proud we are."

3. When it is 9 P.M. in California, what time is it in Utah? In Iowa?

4. Why is it important to know about time zones when you are making a call across the country?

5. If someone in Los Angeles made a phone call at 10 P.M. to her grandmother in North Carolina, how would the grandmother probably react?

6. It is 4 P.M. in New Jersey. If people there started to watch a football game in San Francisco, what time would the game be starting in California?

Life Skills

If you want to sell a bike, get a job, or rent an apartment, you've come to the right place. These stories will help you.

Want Ads

WORDS TO KNOW

want ads (wahnt adz) lists of jobs or things that people want to buy, sell, or rent

classified ads (KLAS-uh-feyed adz) another name for want ads

employers (ehm-PLOY-uhrz) people who hire others to work for money

reward (ree-WAWRD) money or a gift given for the return of something lost

abbreviations (uh-bree-vee-AY-shuhnz) short forms of words used instead of the whole words

Are you looking for a job? Do you want to buy a used stereo? Do you need to sell some used clothing? The **want ads** can help you do all of these things.

Has this ever happened to you? You wanted to find an after-school job. You went into every store where you live. But no one was hiring.

Maybe you wanted to buy a used car. You went to every car lot in town. The cars they had were not what you wanted, or they cost too much.

Maybe you wanted to sell your old bike. You asked all your friends, but nobody wanted to buy a used bike. Nobody knew anyone who wanted to buy one.

Next time this happens to you, don't worry. You can save yourself time. You don't have to run all over town. You don't have to ask everyone you know. Just pick up your local newspaper. Then turn to the want ads.

Maybe you have seen want ads before. Every newspaper has them. They are usually found in one part of the paper. This part is called the **classified ads.** Classified ads is another name for want ads.

Classified ads get their name because they are classified, or grouped, by type. For example, all the ads for jobs are together. All the ads for cars are together. All the ads for apartments are in one place. People can easily find what they're looking for. Many papers list hundreds of ads. Suppose the paper didn't group them. It could take someone hours to find a certain ad. Instead, it usually takes a few minutes.

1. What are want ads?

2. How are want ads divided into groups?

3. Why are want ads divided into groups?

In each group of want ads, the ads are listed in a certain order. That order is by the alphabet. Say you're looking for a job. The job ads would be listed like this. *Auto mechanic* would come before *baker*. *Chef* would come before *dish washer*. *Gardener* would come before *hotel clerk*.

Want ads help bring people together. **Employers** find workers. Buyers find sellers. Apartment owners find renters. Those are just a few examples.

Many other people use the want ads.

Someone looking for work may place an ad. People who can fix things often do this. Someone who has lost something may place an ad. The ad may offer a **reward.** The person who returns the lost thing will get money or a gift. People also place ads to tell about special happenings like sales.

Want ads tell about many things. But all want ads are the same in some ways. They all use **abbreviations.** Certain words are not spelled out. For example, *room* may be written *rm*. This saves space. Want ads cost money. The longer the ad, the more money you pay. Abbreviations save money.

All want ads give details. Job ads tell about jobs. They tell about the experience needed. Car ads give details about the cars being sold. They often tell the price. Apartment ads tell how many rooms there are. They tell what the rent is. They may tell if pets are allowed.

Finally, all want ads list phone numbers or addresses. That is so people can contact whoever placed the ad.

You can learn even more about want ads. Pick up a newspaper. Turn to the want ads. Read them. It doesn't matter if you're not looking for anything now. Someday you will be. Then the want ads will be useful. You'll be very glad you know all about them.

4. In what order are ads listed in each group?

5. Why are abbreviations used in want ads?

6. What details might an ad for an apartment have?

7. Why do want ads have a phone number or address?

Writing a Résumé

WORDS TO KNOW

résumé (REHZ-oo-may) a list of a person's work experience and schooling

qualified (KWAHL-uh-feyed) having the skills and knowledge needed to do a job

applicants (AP-lih-kuhntz) people who try to get a job

interview (IHN-tuhr-vyoo) a meeting in which people ask questions and give answers

summary (SUM-uh-ree) a short list or description of something

When you look for a job, you want to show what you can do. One way to do this is by writing a good **résumé**.

You're excited. You have been looking for a job. You've searched the want ads for days. Now you see a job that's right for you. The job sounds like fun. The pay seems good. You have experience doing this kind of work.

You're ready to call the number in the ad. Then you read it again. Uh-oh. The last line says: *"Please send résumé."* Now you're worried. You're not even sure what a résumé is. How can you send one?

Don't worry. A résumé is a simple thing. It's just a piece of paper. But in the job world, it can be very important.

A résumé is a list of your skills and experience. It tells about your schooling. It tells about jobs you've had. Writing a good résumé is important. It won't help you get a job for which you are not **qualified.** If you don't have the right skills, you won't be hired. But it will help you get a job that's right for you.

1. What is a résumé?

2. For what is a résumé used?

A résumé helps you stand out. Sometimes there are many **applicants** for a job. Many employers are too busy to talk to everyone who wants the job. So they ask for résumés. They read the résumés. Then employers decide whom they want to see. They call just a few people to come for an **interview.** This way employers save time.

An employer may read lots of résumés. Many of them may describe the same kind of work experiences. For example, a restaurant wants to hire a waiter. Most applicants have some experience waiting on tables. How does the employer decide which people to ask for an interview? The ones who have good résumés have the best chance of getting an interview.

Several things make a good résumé. It should be clear and well written. It should be neatly typed. It should have all words spelled correctly. It should tell the truth. Don't make things up just to sound good.

All résumés list certain things. Your name, address, and phone number should be at the top.

You should have a short paragraph next. It should be a **summary** of your skills.

Then tell about your education. List the schools you went to. Tell about any special training you had. Suppose you want a job as an auto mechanic. Write down anything you took in school that could help you in that job.

Next, list the jobs you have had. List the latest job first. Describe the work you did. Then list other jobs you have had. For example, you may want to work in a day care center. Tell about any baby-sitting jobs you've had. These jobs show you can work with children.

Even if you haven't had experience doing a job, don't worry. Many places have on-the-job training. They might hire you without experience. You learn the job while you work. You should still list any jobs you have had. This shows an employer you can be responsible. It shows you will come to work on time. It shows you will do your work carefully.

If you have never had a job, you can still do a résumé. Start with your name, address, and phone number. List your education. Then tell about all your good points. Tell why you would make a good worker. Tell what your goals are. Without work experience, you might not get the first job you want. But sooner or later someone will give you a chance.

Before you do a résumé, take some time. Write down some notes about your past jobs. Then do a "practice" résumé. Show it to someone who knows about résumés. Ask for help in improving it. Then make a final copy. With a good résumé, you're on the way to getting the job you want.

3. Why do employers want résumés?

4. What should you tell about your education?

5. What is the most important thing you should tell about jobs you've had?

6. What should you put on a résumé if you've never had a job?

7. How would you make yourself "stand out" on a résumé?

Job Interview

WORDS TO KNOW

prepared (prih-PAIRD) ready ahead of time for something

impression (ihm-PREHSH-uhn) the strong effect made on someone's feelings and thoughts by an action or event

confident (KAHN-fih-duhnt) sure of yourself

You've applied for the job you've always wanted. Your excellent résumé impressed the employer. Now he or she wants to meet you. Here are some ideas to help you get ready for that important meeting.

The phone rings. It's the call you've been waiting for. Weeks ago you applied for a job. You sent in a résumé. It listed your skills and experience. Since then you have not heard from the company.

Today someone called. She wants you to come in for an interview. She wants to talk with you about your skills. You're excited. You're also worried. You've never been on a job interview before. You don't know what to expect.

It's okay to feel a little worried. People usually feel that way about job interviews. But a job interview doesn't have to be frightening. It can be interesting. It can even be fun. The key is to be **prepared** before you set foot in the door. That way you'll be ready for whatever happens.

First, know what an interview is. An interview is a way for the employer to learn about you. That means you will be asked many questions. It's also a way for you to learn more about the employer. That means you get to ask questions, too.

You will be asked many kinds of questions. But there are a few questions you can count on. One is, "Why do you want this job?" Another is, "Why should I hire you?" You may be asked to tell your good points. You may be asked to tell your weak points, too.

1. What is a job interview?

2. What is one question you can expect on a job interview?

Your answers depend on the job. Why do you want the job in the first place? You should be able to list some reasons. Maybe the work interests you. Maybe it sounds like fun. Maybe you like being around other people. Maybe you need money. All these are reasons people have for working.

There is one answer employers don't want to hear. It's okay to want and need money. But if you give this as your main reason, an employer may think you're not really interested in the job. You should have another reason, too.

Before the interview, think about why you want the job. Write down your reasons. Keep them short. Then practice saying these reasons. Now think about why they should hire you. Write down some good reasons. When the interview comes, you will have the answers in your memory.

Remember, you can ask questions, too. In fact, you should. Think about what's important to you. Do you want to move up to a better job someday? Then ask if that's possible. Do you want to work on weekends? Then ask about that.

Again, it's good to write down your questions before the interview. Bring them with you. Sometimes you won't have to ask them. The employer will tell you the answers first.

At a good interview, many questions are asked. You may be asked about past jobs. You may be asked how you solve problems. You may be asked how well you get along with others. You should always tell the truth. Lying is never a good idea.

Your goal at the interview is to make the best **impression** you can. You want the employer to think well of you. Here are some ways to do that.

Dress well. Be sure your clothes are neat and clean. It doesn't matter what kind of job you've applied for. You should always dress well for an interview.

Be on time or early. Think of the interview as the first day on the job.

Be alert and **confident.** You want to look sure of yourself. Sit up straight. Pay attention. Look at the person asking the questions. Don't speak too fast. Try to act relaxed.

Be yourself. Don't pretend to be someone you're not. If you don't know the answer to a question, say so.

Remember, an interview is a "give and take" thing. You and the employer learn about each other. Each person gives some information. Each person takes some back. In the end, you hope you agree that the job is right for you.

Now you know what to expect in a job interview. It might help you the next time you have one. If you're still nervous, don't worry. Employers understand. They're used to that. Just be yourself. Have a great interview!

3. How can you be ready for questions you might be asked?

4. In all your answers to questions, what is the most important thing you should do?

5. What does the writer mean by saying, "Think of the interview as the first day on the job"?

6. Why do employers not like to hear that a person wants a job because of money?

7. Think of a job you'd like to have. What are two reasons why you want this job?

Finding an Apartment

WORDS TO KNOW

rent (rehnt) to pay money to live someplace

furnished (FUR-nihshd) filled with furniture

unfurnished (uhn-FUR-nihshd) without furniture

landlord (LAND-lawrd) the owner of an apartment or house who rents it to others

lease (lees) an agreement that tells what is expected if you rent an apartment

security deposit (sih-KYOOR-ih-tee dih-PAHZ-iht) money held by the landlord in case of damage

---

Now that you have a good job, this seems like the right time to get a place of your own. Here are some tips on finding an apartment.

Most people who look for a place of their own decide to **rent.** It takes a lot of money money to buy a place to live. If you decide to rent an apartment, think about what you can afford to pay each month.

Start looking for an apartment in the areas you know. Drive or walk through them. Often people put "For Rent" signs out. Ring the door bell to get more information.

You can also ask your friends. Sometimes that's a good way to learn about an apartment before anyone else does.

If you still haven't found the right place, turn to the want ads. The want ads are very good for apartment hunting. Your local newspaper should have many ads. Some ads are for **furnished** apartments. These places come with furniture. Other ads are for **unfurnished** places. These apartments are just empty rooms. The heading above the ads tells you what kind of an apartment it is. Some headings also tell you where the apartment is located.

1. What are three ways to find an apartment?

2. What is a furnished apartment?

3. What is an unfurnished apartment?

Most want ads use abbreviations. For example, *br* stands for *bedroom*. *Kit* stands for *kitchen*. *Utl* stands for *utilities*, such as gas and electricity. *Gar* stands for *garage*.

Most want ads give certain details. They say how big a place is. They say where it is. They tell you what the rent is. They give you a phone number to call.

Suppose the ad doesn't tell you what you want to know. For example, can you have a pet? Write down any questions you have. Then ask them when you call about the place. Get answers before you go see it. It may save you a wasted trip.

Once you've found a few places to check out, think about what to look for in an apartment. Ask yourself questions like these. Do you like the apartment? Is it big enough?

Maybe it's too big. Why pay for more room than you need?

Take a walk through every room. Is the apartment clean? Has it been well kept? If not, will the **landlord,** or owner, clean it before you move in? Are things broken? If so, point them out. They should be fixed before you move in.

Try to picture yourself living there. How much furniture will you need? Is there a stove and refrigerator? If not, you'll have to buy them. Check each room for electrical outlets. Some old apartments have very few. If you have many electrical things, this may be a problem.

If all this seems to be too much to remember, write down these things. Make a list before you see the place. Then check things off as you go along.

At last you have found a place you like. The next step is to fill out an application. This form asks for some facts about you. Where do you live now? Do you pay your bills? Do you have a good job? The application gives the landlord a chance to find out about you.

If your application is accepted, you will have to sign a **lease.** This paper tells what you must do to rent the apartment. For example, you must pay the rent on time. It also tells what the landlord must do. For example, the landlord must fix the things that don't work. The lease tells your rights if you and the landlord have a problem. Be very careful. Read the lease closely before you sign. If you don't understand something, show it to someone who can explain it to you.

Before you can move in, you'll have to pay a month's rent. You'll also probably have to pay a **security deposit.** Sometimes that's another month's rent. The landlord holds this money in case you break something. You get most or all of it back when you move out.

You've signed the lease. You've paid the rent. The landlord has given you the key. Congratulations! You're ready to move in.

4. Tell two things you should check when looking at an apartment.

5. What is a lease?

6. Why must you pay a security deposit?